S0-ABZ-462

FATHER

TERRY

MOTHER

BROTHER

GARDENER

GRANDMA

MAID

LE CHEF

Then the Troll Heard the Squeak

BY KEVIN HAWKES

PUFFIN BOOKS

to Karen

PUFFIN BOOKS   Published by the Penguin Group
Penguin Books USA Inc., 375 Hudson Street, New York, New York 10014, U.S.A.
Penguin Books Ltd, 27 Wrights Lane, London W8 5TZ, England
Penguin Books Australia Ltd, Ringwood, Victoria, Australia
Penguin Books Canada Ltd, 10 Alcorn Avenue, Toronto, Ontario, Canada M4V 3B2
Penguin Books (N.Z.) Ltd, 182–190 Wairau Road, Auckland 10, New Zealand
Penguin Books Ltd, Registered Offices: Harmondsworth, Middlesex, England

First published in the United States of America by Lothrop, Lee & Shepard Books,
a division of William Morrow and Company, Inc., 1991
Reprinted by arrangement with William Morrow and Company, Inc.
Published in Puffin Books, 1992   10 9 8 7 6 5 4 3 2 1
Copyright © Kevin Hawkes, 1991   All rights reserved

LIBRARY OF CONGRESS CATALOGING-IN-PUBLICATION DATA
Hawkes, Kevin.   Then the troll heard the squeak / by Kevin Hawkes.   p.   cm.
Summary: Little Miss Terry wreaks havoc by jumping on the bedsprings at night,
until a troll appears to set things aright.   ISBN 0-14-054469-0
[1. Trolls—Fiction. 2. Behavior—Fiction. 3. Stories in rhyme.] I. Title.
PZ8.3.H288Th   1992   [E]—dc20   92-12528

Printed in the United States of America   Set in Fenice

Except in the United States of America, this book is sold subject to the condition
that it shall not, by way of trade or otherwise, be lent, re-sold, hired out, or otherwise
circulated without the publisher's prior consent in any form of binding or cover other than
that in which it is published and without a similar condition including this condition
being imposed on the subsequent purchaser.

Little Miss Terry
thought it quite merry
to jump on the bedsprings at night.

"Gadzooks!" cried her mother.

"All gone," sighed her brother.

Grandma's new dentures took flight!

The maid took a slip...

...the gardener a clip.

"Oh la la!" cried the cook. "Where's the light?"

Then the troll heard the squeak

and came up for a peek

to set little Miss Terry aright.